What's Maggie Up To?

For
Winifred

Library of Congress Cataloging-in-Publication Data
Bernhard, Durga.
What's Maggie up to? / by Durga Bernhard.
p.   cm.
Summary : The children in an apartment house wonder what the
wandering cat Maggie is up to when she changes her behavior and
disappears into the attic for days.
ISBN 0-8234-0969-4
[1. Cats—Fiction. 2. Apartment houses—Fiction.] I. Title.
PZ7.B44517Wh   1992   91-42915   CIP   AC
[E]—dc20

What's Maggie Up To?

written and illustrated by

Durga Bernhard

Holiday House / New York

Once upon a time, there was
an orange cat named Maggie.

She lived in a big,
sunny apartment house.

In every window, she had a friend.
Mr. Antonio gave her milk in the morning.

Mrs. Bates shared biscuits
with her at teatime.

Beth May introduced her to new friends.

Mrs. Salaz fed her fish for dinner.

Maggie played on windowsills,

tumbled down vines,

and chased mice.

One day, Maggie
began to take things.

She took a ball of yarn,

a stuffed bunny,

and striped socks
from the clothesline.

No one knew why.

Then Maggie disappeared
through the old attic window.

She didn't visit her friends
for three days.

She came out for her milk

but didn't stay for tea.

She rarely had time to play.

Everyone wondered,

what's Maggie up to?

"Let's find out," said all the children, and they made a tower to the attic window.

There they saw, on an
old patchwork quilt . . .

ten little Maggies!